SOMETHING SLEEPING IN THE HALL

A CHARLOTTE ZOLOTOW BOOK
C|Z

These verses are for my father,
with thanks for all of his.

Something Sleeping in the Hall
Copyright © 1985 by Karla Kuskin
Printed in the U.S.A. All rights reserved.
1 2 3 4 5 6 7 8 9 10
First Edition

Library of Congress Cataloging in Publication Data
Kuskin, Karla.
  Something sleeping in the hall.

  (An I can read book)
  "A Charlotte Zolotow book."
  Summary: Poems in a humorous vein about animals.
  1. Children's poetry, American. [1. Humorous
poetry. 2. American poetry] I. Title. II. Series.
PS3561.U79S6 1985   811'.54   82-47721
ISBN 0-06-023633-7
ISBN 0-06-023634-5 (lib. bdg.)

An I Can Read Book®

SOMETHING SLEEPING

IN THE HALL

POEMS BY
KARLA KUSKIN

Harper & Row, Publishers

I would like to have a pet,

any kind will do.

I would like to have a pet

exactly like you.

My bird is small.

My bird is shy.

It does not sing.

It cannot fly.

It does no tricks

and that is fine.

I love my bird.

My bird is mine.

There is a tree

that grows in me,

a tree

that no one else can see.

9

There is a bird

upon the tree,

upon the tree

that grows in me.

The tree that no one else can see.

And when the bird

upon the tree

begins to sing,

you think it's me.

There is a fence

around our house.

There is a catbird

on the fence.

12

The catbird will not tie his shoes.

If birds wore shoes

this might make sense.

13

Blue bird on a branch.

Big bird on a twig.

Red bird on a ranch.

Wild bird on a wig.

Broad bird on a bench.

Bored bird on a pig.

Third bird in a bunch.

Blurred bird does a jig.

Do you hear the parrot squawk?

He's talking to

a celery stalk.

The parrot likes to squawk and shout

and throw a lot of seeds about.

One jay

two jay

kitty got a blue jay.

18

Three jay

four jay

there isn't any more jay.

19

When our cat

goes to work or dance,

he wears a pair of soft black pants.

20

He wears a matching shirt
and vest.

two ears that match

the soft black rest,

one matching tail,

four matching feet.

Our cat is slim and trim
and neat.

There was a mouse

who used to sit

about the house

all day and knit

until the cat

got wind of it.

24

The cat

and all her little kittens

came and ate

that mouse's mittens.

I have a little guppy.

I would rather have a puppy.

The running dogs begin to bark

in the morning early.

Their ears blow back,

their tails are flags,

long and short and curly.

My dog runs down the hall

to fetch the ball

and bring it back to me

so I can throw it down the hall

so he can run and fetch the ball

and...

Rabbits

don't like rabbit stew.

32

I don't blame them much,

do you?

There was a hog

who ate a dog

and then he ate

a grass-green frog

34

and then he was so full
he cried.

And then he lay down—

bang—

and died.

A wizard

had a lizard.

They really were a team.

36

The wizard

loved the lizard.

The lizard loved ice cream.

A bear went walking

down the street

and everyone that bear did meet

that bear did greet

and also eat.

How sweet.

BURP

The bear coat

is a hair coat,

a coat of fur

to make bears purrr.

GRRRRR

But bears don't purrr.

They grrrrr.

Compare the bears.

This one has hairs.

This one has none.

Come,

pair the bears.

The sound of a toad

in the road

in the mud

is a soft sort of thump

and a very wet thud.

It makes me squirm

to watch a worm.

Spiders are all right, I guess,

or would be

if their legs were less.

50

I am watering the plants.

I'm also watering the ants.

51

Smoke comes out of the dragon's nose.

Claws come out of

the dragon's toes.

Flames

flame from the dragon's mouth,

east and west

and north and south.

Look,

here comes an awful dragon.

Wait,

I think his tail is wagging.

The dragon walks

for miles and miles.

He eats up people.

Then he smiles.

The dragon smiles

because he knows

that nothing tastes as good

as toes.

The lion looks extremely proud.

58

But when he eats,

he chews too loud.

The deer is fine and fleet

when leaping,

but she is just a dear

when sleeping.

61

I would like to have a pet,

any kind at all.

Something big,

something small,

62

something sleeping in the hall

would be just fine.

I would like to have a pet.

Will you be mine?

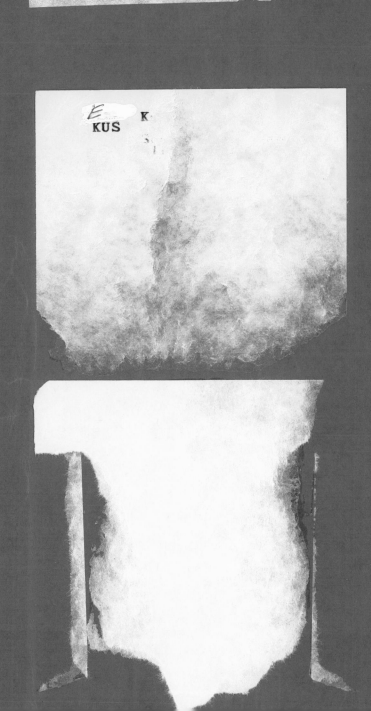